This book belongs to

_____

_____

_____

_____

Shampooch

An original concept by author Heather Pindar
© Heather Pindar
Illustrated by Susan Batori

MAVERICK ARTS PUBLISHING LTD
Studio 3A, City Business Centre, 6 Brighton Road, Horsham,
West Sussex, RH13 5BB, +44 (0)1403 256941
© Maverick Arts Publishing Limited
Published January 2019

A CIP catalogue record for this book
is available at the British Library.

ISBN 978-1-84886-381-1

www.maverickbooks.co.uk

SHAMPOOCH

Written by
Heather Pindar

Illustrated by
Susan Batori

It only took 3 hours and 42 minutes at the Furaway Dog Pampering Salon; shampoo, cut, blow-dry, nose polish, claw-buffing, tail-fluffing and whisker gloss.

Diamanté collar on, designer mohair jacket perfectly fitted and...

...she was ready.

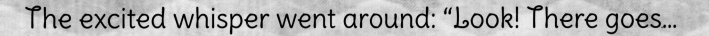
The excited whisper went around: "Look! There goes...

...Shampooch!"

"I feel fabulous! My fur's silkier than ever," she said.
"And now for the park, it's the place to be seen."

"Good dog, clean dog," said her humans.
"Take care, Shampooch! Don't go too far."

Daintily, Shampooch began to climb the big, breezy hill.

"Shampooch! Come and play in the rubbish bins,"
barked Wagsy McBone. "They're lovely and stinky today."

"No, thanks, Wagsy, I've just had my tail fluffed."

"Yo, Shampooch! Want to roll in the mud patch?" panted Woof-Whiffily.

"No, thanks, Woofy, I don't want to be a dirty dog."

"Hey, Shampooch!" panted Sniffy-Bottingham. "Want to chase rabbits in the scraggly bushes?"

"In *this* collar? I don't think so, Sniffy!" said Shampooch.

Leaving a waft of 'Le Chien' perfume behind her,
she stepped over the brow of the breezy hill.

"Oooh," breathed Shampooch, "That's...

...beautiful!"

But suddenly SOMETHING BIG rattled loudly and...

...THWOCKED

Shampooch **high** in the air...

...and skittered her down the breezy hill.

Shampooch *hurtled* through the scraggly bushes.

Shampooch *slithered* across the mud patch.

Kerplonk!

Bump, bump, "Aiooooo!"

Shampooch *flumped* into the rubbish bins.

"Ai yi-yiiii!" yelped Shampooch.

"Oh my! That was really...

... Let's do it all again!"

"*Bad* dogs! *Dirty* dogs! Home to bed!" said their humans.

"Has anyone seen a big, clean, silky dog with a freshly-fluffed tail?" panted Shampooch's humans rushing forwards. "We can't find her *anywhere*."

"'Fraid not," said Sniffy's human, "there's just these naughty dogs here."

"Ruff-ruff!" yelped Shampooch. "Ruff-ruff, ro-ro!"

"Shampooch! At last!" cried her humans. "We've found...

...EWWWWWW!"